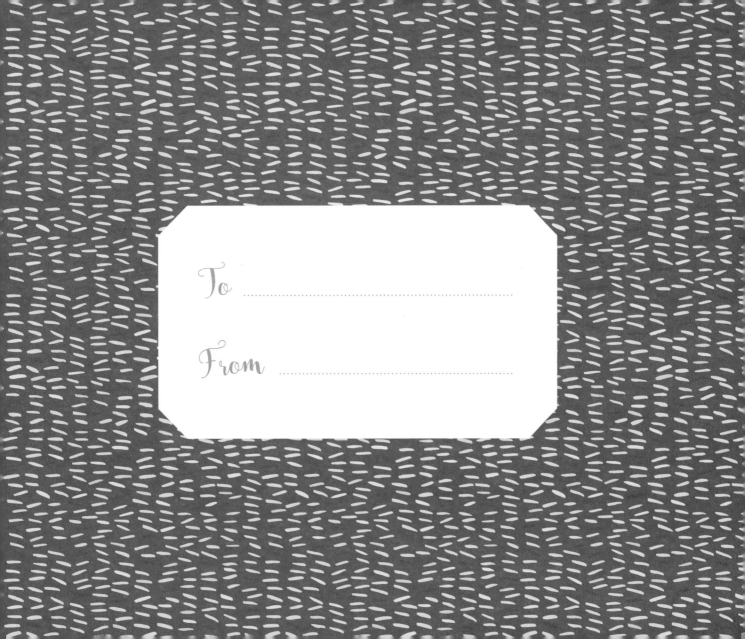

To .....................................................

From .....................................................

Published by Cumberland House, an imprint of Sourcebooks, Inc.
P.O. Box 4410, Naperville, Illinois 60567-4410
(630) 961-3900
Fax: (630) 961-2168
sourcebooks.com

Printed and bound in China.
PP 10 9 8 7 6 5 4 3 2 1

# WHY a DAUGHTER NEEDS a MOM

GREGORY E. LANG

CUMBERLAND HOUSE™

# A DAUGHTER
# NEEDS A MOM

*to love her for*

*who she is*

A DAUGHTER NEEDS A MOM

*to give her*

THE COURAGE TO

*stand up for herself*

A DAUGHTER
NEEDS A MOM

to catch her if

she falls

A daughter
needs a mom

To show her how to use
humor to lighten heavy loads.

. . . . . . . . . . .

To show her how to put a little
love in everything she does.

. . . . . . . . . . .

To tell her not to let pride get
in the way of forgiving someone.

A DAUGHTER
NEEDS A MOM

*to indulge her*

*individuality*

A daughter
needs a mom

To teach her how to look her best.

. . . . . . . . . . . .

Who can read the expression on her face.

. . . . . . . . . . . .

Who shares with her the wisdom of generations.

A DAUGHTER NEEDS A MOM

*to teach her*

THAT EVERY TREE TAKES

*a while to grow*

A daughter
needs a mom

To read to her.

...........

Who wants to help make her
wishes come true.

...........

To remind her, on the bad days,
that she is not alone.

A DAUGHTER NEEDS A MOM

*to remind her*

THAT THERE IS A RAINBOW

*after every storm*

A DAUGHTER NEEDS A MOM

to point out that there

IS A DIFFERENCE BETWEEN BEING

adventurous and being wild

# A DAUGHTER
# NEEDS A MOM

*to teach her
not to be afraid to
seize the moment*

A DAUGHTER
NEEDS A MOM

*to help her on
her wedding day*

A daughter needs a mom

To prepare her for what she will face
when she leaves home.

· · · · · · · · · · ·

To teach her how to distinguish
the difference between love and lust.

A DAUGHTER NEEDS A MOM

*to remind her*

THAT SHE IS RESPONSIBLE FOR

*her own happiness*

A daughter
needs a mom

To teach her how to
care for children.

.............

To remind her to say nice things
when she talks to herself.

.............

To teach her that women
are not bound to the home.

A DAUGHTER
NEEDS A MOM

to nurture her
imagination

# A DAUGHTER
# NEEDS A MOM

*to teach her how to make thankfulness a habit*

A daughter needs a mom

To listen closely to what troubles her.

. . . . . . . . . . .

To tell her that grudges are
too burdensome to carry.

. . . . . . . . . . .

To teach her that she should
know herself better than anyone else does.

# A DAUGHTER
# NEEDS A MOM

*to teach her to lift*

*her voice in praise*

A daughter

needs a mom

To soothe the pain of a broken heart.

. . . . . . . . . . . .

Who believes it is okay to
see things differently.

. . . . . . . . . . . .

To teach her that you cannot
make someone love you, but you
can be someone who can be loved.

A DAUGHTER NEEDS A MOM

*to tell her*

THAT THE ROAD TO HAPPINESS

*is not always straight*

A daughter
needs a mom

Who does not lose her identity
in the role of wife and mother.

. . . . . . . . . . . .

Who will sing along with her when her
favorite song comes on the radio.

. . . . . . . . . . . .

Who shows by example that
community involvement is a worthy pursuit.

A DAUGHTER NEEDS A MOM

to remind her that she has

THE RIGHT TO INDULGE

herself every now and then

A DAUGHTER NEEDS A MOM

*to challenge her to strive for*
*what is just beyond her reach*

A DAUGHTER
NEEDS A MOM
*to make sure she*
*keeps a true heart*

A daughter
needs a mom

Who is never more than a phone call away.

. . . . . . . . . . .

Because no one understands
girls like a mom.

. . . . . . . . . . .

To explain that the sweetest flower
may not always be the prettiest.

A DAUGHTER NEEDS A MOM

*to remind her*

THAT IN FAITH THERE

*is fellowship*

A daughter
needs a mom

To show her the comfort
of a warm embrace.

. . . . . . . . . . . .

To encourage her to laugh
as often as possible.

. . . . . . . . . . . .

To teach her not to wait until
tomorrow to say, "I'm sorry."

A DAUGHTER NEEDS A MOM

*to teach her*

THAT THE PATH TAKEN IS AS

*important as the destination*

# A daughter needs a mom

To sing her to sleep.

. . . . . . . . . . .

Who never grows tired
of holding hands.

. . . . . . . . . . .

Who knows how to put
a smile on her face.

A daughter
needs a mom

To carry her when she is tired.

. . . . . . . . . . . .

To show her how
to give back to others.

. . . . . . . . . . . .

To help her see that
death is a part of life.

# A DAUGHTER
# NEEDS A MOM

*to give her
the freedom to
express herself*

A daughter
needs a mom

To encourage her to be grateful.

. . . . . . . . . . .

To show her how to make
use of what she already has.

. . . . . . . . . . .

To share in her excitement
when she falls in love for the first time.

A DAUGHTER NEEDS A MOM

*to teach her*

NOT TO LET A GOOD DAY

*slip from her fingers*

A daughter
needs a mom

To show her how to raise a family.

. . . . . . . . . . . .

To teach her that even
true love requires compromise.

. . . . . . . . . . . .

To teach her to love
her friends, no matter what they do.

# A DAUGHTER
# NEEDS A MOM

*to share in*

*her daydreams*

A DAUGHTER NEEDS A MOM

*to remind her to be playful,*
*no matter how old she is*

A DAUGHTER NEEDS A MOM

*to provide her*

WITH MEMORIES THAT

*last forever*

A DAUGHTER
NEEDS A MOM

because without her she
will have less in her
life than she deserves